J. T Yarrington

The Omnium-Gatherum

The American Fortune-Teller

J. T Yarrington

The Omnium-Gatherum
The American Fortune-Teller

ISBN/EAN: 9783337371401

Printed in Europe, USA, Canada, Australia, Japan

Cover: Foto ©Andreas Hilbeck / pixelio.de

More available books at **www.hansebooks.com**

The Omnium-Gatherum;

or,

The American Fortune-Teller:

AN AMUSEMENT FOR

Parties and the Social Circle.

Entered according to Act of Congress, in the year 1872, by
J. T. YARRINGTON,
In the office of the Librarian of Congress, at Washington.

CARBONDALE, PA.

PUBLISHED AND SOLD BY J. T. YARRINGTON.

Price, Fifty Cents.

ALSO FOR SALE AT ALL BOOKSTORES, AND BY NEWS-AGENTS
AND DEALERS IN FANCY GOODS, TOYS, GAMES, ETC.,
THROUGHOUT THE UNITED STATES AND CANADAS.

THE OMNIUM-GATHERUM;

OR,

The American Fortune-Teller.

A NEW GAME FOR THE YOUNG.

BY J. T. YARRINGTON.

EXPLANATION.—THE OMNIUM-GATHERUM is designed, principally, for the young—to amuse the boys and girls; however, older people, with young hearts, may join in the game, and find some merriment in it, particularly when accompanied by our youthful friends.

There are eighteen questions, and thirty-eight various answers to each separate question, all numbered respectively from one to thirty-eight.

Let one of the company act as interrogator, or reader. He or she will ask the questions in regular order, as laid down in the game. Begin with one person, and finish his or her "fortune" before commencing with that of another.

Each time the reader asks a question, the candidate, or party so interrogated, will call off a stated number, aloud, (said number not to exceed thirty-eight,) and the questioner will then read the answer to that number. So on through.

The ODD numbers are arranged for MALES, and the EVEN numbers for FEMALES, always. It is important that this be borne in mind, so that all the answers shall be appropriate for each sex. Let the reader see to this matter, that no wrong numbers are given, and then no mistakes will occur in rendering answers to the several questions.

It is hoped, and the earnest desire of the compiler is, that the OMNIUM-GATHERUM will prove a pleasant fireside game, an innocent yet happy diversion for both young and old; that this game will be, truly, an amusement for parties and the social circle, what it is designed to be; that tens of thousands of our American boys and girls, all over the land, who shall indulge in this play, may live to grow up to noble manhood and womanhood, enter life's battle-field in earnest, go forth to do valiant service for God and humanity, engage in the temperance and other reformatory enterprises of the age, be bright and shining lights in the world, an honor to their country, and promoters of her morals, principles, peace and universal freedom!

Yours, in behalf of law and

liberty, moral and political,

J. T. YARRINGTON.

FIRST QUESTION.

WHAT IS YOUR FORTE, OR HIGHEST AMBITION?

NO.	ANSWER.

1. To speculate in stocks.
2. To distribute to the poor.
3. To drive a fast nag.
4. To receive calls.
5. To flatter the girls.
6. To teach a school.
7. To keep a livery stable.
8. To dress in the latest style.
9. To flirt with young ladies.
10. To excel in music.
11. To own a pea-nut stand.
12. To cultivate personal charms.
13. To be very rich.
14. To travel in foreign lands.
15. To raise a nice moustache.
16. To win admiration.
17. To marry a handsome brunette.

18. To have plenty of beaux.

19. To do good in the world.

20. To be a favorite among folks.

21. To acquire great fame.

22. To love everybody.

23. To secure political preferment.

24. To oppose all wrong.

25. To receive a liberal education.

26. To become distinguished.

27. To have the smiles of Nancy.

28. To please superiors.

29. To earn an honest living.

30. To be with Charlie, often.

31. To observe and learn of others.

32. To put the best side out.

33. To plague associates.

34. To be a milliner.

35. To achieve great renown for morals.

36. To live in a brown stone-mansion.

37. To be a bank president.

38. To attract attention.

SECOND QUESTION.

WHAT IS THE MOST REMARKABLE THING YOU EVER SAW, OR HEARD?

NO.   ANSWER.

1. Nellie's indifference about marriage.
2. Cupid's whisperings.
3. The girl of the period.
4. An English swell.
5. The Grecian bend.
6. A contented bachelor.   ·
7. A coquette in love.
8. An essay on single blessedness.
9. The song of the fairies.
10. A cat concert.
11. A silent kiss.
12. Friendship between rivals.
13. A Scotch bag-pipe.
14. A fly trap.
15. An infuriated monster.
16. A liberal millionaire.
17. An ancient town clock.

18. A perfumed dandy.

19. Molasses pie.

20. A swearing parrot.

21. A lecture on "bumpology."

22. A quaker-meeting.

23. An Indian pow-wow.

24. A fish without eyes.

25. An eclipse.

26. A storm at sea.

27. Genius undeveloped.

28. Pride without possessions.

29. Beauty unadorned.

30. A jug without a handle.

31. Mixing oil with water.

32. A story well told.

33. A law against finery.

34. Fashion and famine.

35. "Ask mamma."

36. A velocipede.

37. A goose that wouldn't hiss.

38. A proposal of marriage.

THIRD QUESTION.

WHERE DO YOU FIND PLEASURE, OR HAPPINESS?

NO.   ANSWER.

1. In studying.
2. At work.
3. When in the discharge of duty.
4. In reflection.
5. At home.
6. With personal friends.
7. By the side of Jerusha.
8. At a reception.
9. In the "little church around the corner."
10. In the country.
11. At Saratoga.
12. On the mountains.
13. In the workshop.
14. In the glen.
15. On the ocean.
16. 'Neath the willows.
17. Where there are winsome young ladies.

18. In the flower-garden.
19. On the ice.
20. Horse-back riding.
21. At a clam-bake.
22. At a social hop.
23. In the harvest field.
24. At singing-school.
25. At a " mutual admiration society."
26. In the city.
27. In the employ of Venus..
28. In the sanctuary.
29. In the store, selling goods.
30. In a palace coach, traveling.
31. At a woman's rights convention.
32. At a musical festival.
33. At an apple-cut.
34. In the sewing circle.
35. At a masquerade carnival.
36. At a wedding.
37. At neighbor Blank's.
38. In a baby show.

FOURTH QUESTION.

WHAT DO YOU MOST DESIRE?

NO.   ANSWER.

1. A new suit of clothes.
2. A thousand-dollar piano.
3. Peace and plenty.
4. To be married.
5. A villa on the Hudson.
6. The latest novel.
7. Turkey for dinner.
8. An interview with Harry.
9. A silk hat.
10. To see the queen.
11. A chat with Sally.
12. To be a belle.
13. A gold watch.
14. To see London.
15. A pair of pet rabbits.
16. A pleasant surprise.
17. A tour through the Holy Land.
18. To be handsome.

19. To be a prince.
20. A set of jewelry.
21. An independent fortune.
22. Health and happiness.
23. To please the fair sex.
24. The society of young gentlemen.
25. A large farm, well stocked.
26. A horse and carriage.
27. The plaudits of wise men.
28. The confidence of associates.
29. To increase in knowledge.
30. To display finery.
31. Faith and fortitude.
32. Paint and powder.
33. Sweetness, personified.
34. The beginning of better days.
35. Prohibition of the dram-shop.
36. The reign of charity.
37. The accumulation of property.
38. Many friends, no enemies.

FIFTH QUESTION.

WHAT QUALITY, ACCOMPLISHMENT OR PECULIAR CHARACTERISTIC DO YOU WISH IN YOUR PARTNER FOR LIFE?

NO.   ANSWER.

1. Domestic felicity.
2. Courage.
3. Maternal kindness.
4. Contentment.
5. General intelligence.
6. Literary aspirations.
7. Cheerfulness.
8. Generosity.
9. Loving disposition.
10. Mirthfulness.
11. An early riser.
12. Sense and wit.
13. Well versed in etiquette.
14. Good manners.
15. A refined mind.

16. Ingenuity.
17. Royal ancestry.
18. Dignity.
19. Fine form and features.
20. Government bonds.
21. Amiability.
22. Superior attainments.
23. Great musical talent.
24. Gentility.
25. Truthfulness.
26. Temperate habits.
27. Wealth.
28. Industry.
29. Beauty.
30. Education.
31. Blue eyes.
32. Religion.
33. Order.
34. Activity.
35. Compassion.
36. Economy.
37. Modesty.
38. Honesty.

SIXTH QUESTION.

WITH WHOM HAVE YOU EVER BEEN IN LOVE?

NO.   ANSWER.

1. A fascinating damsel.
2. A gay cavalier.
3. The Senator's daughter.
4. A lawyer.
5. A dressmaker.
6. The son of a millionaire.
7. A Scotch lassie.
8. A jolly old Teuton.
9. An eccentric old maid.
10. A widower worth $50,000.
11. A lady of high rank.
12. A gentleman of color.
13. Tim's sister.
14. An English fop.
15. A public singer.
16. A cobbler.
17. An actress.

18. A crazy sycophant.

19. The maid of the forest.

20. A fine old gent of sixty summers.

21. A gipsy girl.

22. A marriageable bachelor.

23. A fat, lazy widow.

24. A good-looking soldier.

25. A gossiping chatter-box.

26. A backwoodsman.

27. An angel in disguise.

28. A locomotive engineer.

29. One whom you will yet marry.

30. A New York merchant.

31. A pert little miss.

32. A quack doctor.

33. A certain married lady.

34. A clergyman.

35. A bouncing country girl.

36. A noted land agent.

37. A spinster.

38. A Chinaman.

SEVENTH QUESTION.

WHAT ARE YOU THINKING ABOUT?

NO.	ANSWER.

1. The grand result of all.
2. The young man you love.
3. Fashion's foibles.
4. The wheel of fortune.
5. The decrees of fate.
6. Last night's promenade.
7. Junie's invitation.
8. The forthcoming party.
9. Mary's sly glances.
10. Whom to invite to the wedding.
11. When to "pop the question."
12. Of how much money he has got.
13. Her answer, "No," or "Yes,"
14. The excursion next week.
15. How to win her affections.
16. Why he don't call again.
17. Lizzie's numerous lovers.
18. Life after marriage.

19. Christmas presents.

20. The honeymoon.

21. Where to go on a wedding tour.

22. The coming man.

23. The stolen kiss.

24. Flirting with the gents.

25. Her delightful ways.

26. Man's inconsistency.

27. Girlish devotion.

28. Love, courtship and marriage.

29. The choice to make.

30. The engagements of the week.

31. How much to pay the minister.

32. The flattery of men.

33. The prospects for success.

34. What to wear to the opera.

35. A pair of bright eyes.

36. The trials of an old maid.

37. The pleasures of youth.

38. Where to spend the season.

EIGHTH QUESTION.

BY WHOM ARE YOU GREATLY ADMIRED?

NO.   ANSWER.

1. A talkative lady.

2. A perfect gentleman.

3. A cross-eyed woman.

4. A pack peddler.

5. A great beauty.

6. An auctioneer.

7. A stylish coquette.

8. A squinting physician.

9. A widow with fifteen children.

10. A man who has had three wives.

11. A dame of seventy years.

12. A tailor.

13. A dress-maker.

14. A dry-goods merchant.

15. A lady of fortune and fame.

16. A bank clerk.

17. An old washer-woman.

18. A romance writer.

19. A street flirt.
20. The priest.
21. An irritable young lady.
22. A city druggist.
23. A modern duchess.
24. A real estate agent.
25. A scolding prude.
26. A mulatto man.
27. A hotel servant girl.
28. A rag picker.
29. An editress of a magazine.
30. A minstrel performer.
31. A seminary student.
32. A dentist.
33. An exquisite demoiselle.
34. An omnibus driver.
35. A seamstress.
36. A green grocer.
37. A girl whom you never met.
38. A lazy fellow.

NINTH QUESTION.

FOR WHAT ARE YOU LOVED, OR WHY?

NO.	ANSWER.
1.	For your qualities of heart and mind.
2.	For your social, pleasant ways.
3.	Because you favor the ladies.
4.	For your peculiar style.
5.	For your generosity.
6	Because you are brave and true.
7.	For your firmness of character.
8.	For your conversational powers.
9.	Because you are obliging.
10.	For your natural talents.
11.	For your many virtues.
12.	Because you know how to please.
13.	For your good disposition.
14.	For your small hands and feet.
15.	Because you are industrious.
16.	For your personal charms.
17.	For your strict morals.
18.	Because you excel in music.

19. For your business tact.

20. For your modesty.

21. Because you are humorous.

22. For your worldly possessions.

23. For your pecuniary prospects.

24. For your accomplishments.

25. Because you are irresistible.

26 For your nameless attractions.

27. For your faultless form.

28. Because you are cheerful.

29. For your Roman nose.

30. For your liberal views.

31. Because you are charitable.

32. For your smiling features.

33. For your eminent ability.

34 For your rustic simplicity.

35. For your extreme good nature.

36. For your dispassionate temper.

37. For your moderate desires.

38. For your labors of mercy and peace.

TENTH QUESTION.

WHEN, OR WHERE, WILL YOU FIRST MEET YOUR INTENDED?

NO.   ANSWER.

1. At an agricultural fair.
2. At a passenger depot.
3. On the banks of a river.
4. At the opera.
5. At a moonlight serenade.
6. In a beautiful glen.
7. On Niagara suspension bridge.
8. At the wedding of a friend.
9. In a fashion-store.
10. In a flower-garden.
11. At church.
12. In an omnibus.
13. On the crowded thoroughfare.
14. Next summer, or autumn.
15. In a drug-store.
16. At a picture-gallery.
17. In the kitchen, washing dishes.

18. At a social meeting.

19. At her residence.

20. On the seashore.

21. At the theatre.

22. In a city park.

23. At the seminary.

24. At a soiree.

25. At a village gathering.

26. On board a steamer.

27. At a fancy ball.

28. In a select company.

29. At a large hotel.

30. At a camp-meeting.

31. At a concert.

32. At his parents' home.

33. At a menagerie and circus.

34. At a charity festival.

35. In the cars.

36. At a pic-nic.

37. In an ice-cream restaurant.

38. At a museum.

ELEVENTH QUESTION.

WHAT IS HIS, OR HER, GIVEN NAME?

NO.   ANSWER.

1. Viola.
2. Obadiah.
3. Abigail.
4. Aaron.
5. Lizzie.
6. Sylvester.
7. Josephine.
8. Zaccheus.
9. Ella.
10. Theodore.
11. Mary.
12. Elisha.
13. Agnes.
14. Horace.
15. Edith.
16. Samuel.
17. Cornelia.
18. John.

19. Victoria.
20. Martin.
21. Charlotte.
22. Benjamin.
23. Nellie.
24. Levi.
25. Olive.
26. Thomas.
27. Maud.
28. Eugene.
29. Carrie.
30. Albert.
31. Virginia.
32. Henry.
33. Sarah.
34. William.
35. Blanche.
36. Jeremiah.
37. Leura.
38. Daniel.

TWELFTH QUESTION.

AT WHAT AGE WILL YOU GET MARRIED

NO.   ANSWER.

1. In your twenty-fifth year.
2. In your fifteenth year.
3. In your forty-first year.
4. In your seventy-sixth year.
5. In your nineteenth year.
6. In your twenty-third year.
7. In your fiftieth year.
8. In your sixty-fourth year.
9. In your thirty-eighth year.
10. In your fifty-fifth year.
11. In your ninetieth year.
12. In your twenty-eighth year.
13. In your twenty-sixth year.
14. In your fifty-seventh year.
15. In your fortieth year.
16. In your nineteenth year.
17. In your fifteenth year.
18. In your twenty-fifth year.

19. In your twenty-ninth year.

20. In your forty-first year.

21. In your seventy-sixth year.

22. In your twenty-ninth year.

23. In your eighty-fourth year.

24. In your forty-seventh year.

25. In your twenty-third year.

26. In your thirty-fifth year.

27. In your thirty-sixth year.

28. In your forty-second year.

29. In your seventeenth year.

30. In your sixteenth year.

31. In your sixty-fourth year.

32. In your fortieth year.

33. In your fifty-seventh year.

34. In your fiftieth year.

35. In your twenty-eighth year.

36. In your thirty-eighth year.

37. In your fifty-fifth year.

38. In your twenty-sixth year.

THIRTEENTH QUESTION.

WHEN WILL THE WEDDING TAKE PLACE?

NO.	ANSWER.

1. On the bride's birthday.
2. On the Fourth of July.
3. On the last day of winter.
4. On New Year's morning.
5. At midnight.
6. On Saint Patrick's day.
7. The first Tuesday in September.
8. Nine o'clock, Sabbath morning.
9. On a cold, stormy day.
10. On May-day.
11. On the President's inaugural day.
12. Two years from date.
13. At sunrise.
14. On Robert Burns' natal day.
15. On a cold, frosty morning.
16. Next summer.
17. On Thanksgiving day.

18. November 30th, 1900.

19. On a fine, autumnal day.

20. Monday, if it don't rain.

21. As soon as she states the time.

22. When his parents consent.

23. On Saint Valentine's day.

24. On the last day of the year.

25. On the eighteenth of June.

26. In mid-winter.

27. On Washington's natal day.

28. On Christmas eve.

29. On all-fool's day.

30. On a bright, moonlight night.

31. On a mild, winter day.

32. Half-past two, Thursday afternoon.

33. On Saint John's day.

34. On the first day of spring.

35. At even-tide.

36. About the middle of December.

37. On the bridegroom's birthday.

38. On a clear, summer morning.

FOURTEENTH QUESTION.

WHERE WILL THE NUPTIALS COME OFF?

NO.   ANSWER.

1. In the cellar.
2. In a pleasant grove.
3. At the county poor-house.
4. In a brick house.
5. At the bride's parents' residence.
6. On the deck of a steamship.
7. On a hill styled Beautiful Mount.
8. In a straw factory.
9. At a large hotel.
10. At a celebrated watering place.
11. On the banks of a famous lake.
12. In a dell called Lovers' Retreat.
13. In a school-house.
14. In an ancient castle.
15. In a pleasant woods.
16. In the cook's apartments.
17. In an Indian wigwam.
18. On a sail-boat.

19. In an old building.
20. At the church.
21. Up garret.
22. In a handsome villa.
23. At a musical convention.
24. In a floral palace.
25. In the wilderness.
26. In a modern cave.
27. In a stone mansion.
28. On a canal boat.
29. In an obscure part of the city.
30. Among strangers.
31. At a private assembly.
32. At a tea-party.
33. In a pine forest.
34. In a cathedral.
35. In an alderman's office.
36. In the open air.
37. In the house of a friend.
38. At the parsonage.

FIFTEENTH QUESTION.

WHAT WILL OCCUR AFTER THE CERE-MONY IS PERFORMED ?

NO.	ANSWER.

1. The bride will be kissed by the parson.

2. A disappointed lover will faint.

3. The bridegroom will refuse to pay the fee.

4. The happy swain will shout for joy.

5. The old folks will give advice.

6. The fowls will begin their concert, and mark time.

7. An old maid will sneeze three times.

8. Grandma will make you a present.

9. The wine will be ordered taken off the table.

10. You will be tendered a grand reception.

11. You will be jealous of your wife.

12. You will be serenaded by friends.

13. Some comrade will offer to take your place.

14. Young ladies will compliment your husband.

15. A bachelor chum will present you with a cradle.

16. A book agent will offer a treatise on divorce.

17. Your mother-in-law will deliver a speech.

18. The servants will cry because you leave home.

19. You will scold your wife.

20. Your husband will want the knot untied.

21. Your friends will criticise your appearance.

22. You will receive $1,000 in gold.

23. A song, "The Bachelor's Lament," will be sung.

24. Your husband will drop his wig, accidentally.

25. Your washerwoman will give you a call.

26. The contents of a large band-box will be disclosed.

27. A collection will be taken to pay expenses.

28. Numerous valuable gifts will be bestowed on you.

29. Grotesque scenes will be enacted.

30. You will learn the value of the gridiron.

31. Music on a jews-harp, by an expert.

32. A parrot will repeat the marriage vows.

33. You will become accustomed to the use of pins.

34. Flattery and soft sawder will abound.

35. You will hear bells, whistles, tin pans, etc.

36. A banquet of peace, plenty and pleasure.

37. You will discover that your wife is *not an angel.*

38. Nothing to mar the joy and comfort of any.

WHAT LUXURY, EXTRAORDINARY, WILL BE PROVIDED FOR THE HAPPY OCCASION ?

NO.   ANSWER.

1. Acorn nectar.
2. Waffles.
3. Boiled eggs.
4. Sour krout.
5. Souse.
6. Lemonade.
7. Artichokes.
8. Sweet potatoes.
9. Figs.
10. Sandwiches.
11. Catnip tea.
12. Johnny cake.
13. Cold water.
14. Gingerbread.
15. Crackers.
16. Asparagus.

17. Sausage.

18. Ice-cream.

19. Dutch cheese.

20. Oysters.

21. Codfish.

22. Chocolate coffee.

23. Baked apples.

24. Cocoanut cake.

25. Soup.

26. Plum pudding.

27. Mush and milk.

28. Pumpkin pie.

29. Buckwheat cakes.

30. Fresh fish.

31. Red herring.

32. Green peas.

33. Crab-apple jelly.

34. Boiled corn.

35. Pork and beans.

36. Turkey.

37. Roast beef.

38. Bread and molasses.

SEVENTEENTH QUESTION.

WHERE WILL YOU GO FOR A WEDDING TOUR?

NO.	ANSWER.

1. To Australia.
2. To Niagara Falls.
3. To Washington.
4. To the Holy Land.
5. To Canada.
6. To Newport.
7. To New Foundland.
8. To New York, Philadelphia and Boston.
9. Over the sea.
10. To London.
11. To Long Branch.
12. To Paris.
13. To the White Mountains.
14. To Florida.
15. To Mexico.
16. To the Isle of Wight.
17. To the British Provinces.

18. To the Wyoming Valley, Pennsylvania.
19. To California, *via* the Union Pacific Railroad.
20. To Rome.
21. To South America.
22. To Nova Scotia.
23. To Charleston.
24. To Chicago and Saint Louis.
25. To the South Sea Islands.
26. To the North Pole.
27. To Scotland.
28. To Kentucky.
29. To Lake Superior.
30. To Dundaff.
31. To New Brunswick.
32. To Detroit.
33. To Japan.
34. To Liverpool.
35. To Nicaragua.
36. Around the world.
37. To Cape May.
38. To China.

WHAT WILL BE THE MOST PROMINENT EVENT OF YOUR MARRIED CAREER?

NO.   ANSWER.

1. Your failure in business.

2. Your exit from home.

3. A legacy from France.

4. The wedding.

5. Your sojourn at your father-in-law's.

6. The death of your husband.

7. Your speculation in oil-stock.

8. Your second marriage.

9. Being turned out of doors by your children.

10. The introduction of a stranger in your circle.

11. The accomplishment of a cherished project.

12. The celebration of your golden wedding.

13. A visit to the old world.

14. Mischief produced by gossip.

15. Your wife's sudden estrangement.

16. Leaving the place of your nativity.

17. Your purchase of real estate in Philadelphia.

18. Immense wealth in after life.
19. The invention of a paying patent.
20. An effort to rule your household.
21. Insubordination in the family.
22. Lecturing before the public.
23. Signing the pledge of total abstinence.
24. Attending a royal banquet.
25. Loss of property by fire.
26. Teaching school and boarding 'round.
27. Cheating your creditors.
28. A valuable discovery made in 1890.
29. Desertion by your wife.
30. The day you become a legal voter.
31. Paying your debts.
32. Demanding your husband's money.
33. Nursing the children.
34. Jealousy, on the part of your husband.
35. Attempting to kiss a handsome girl.
36. Earning a living for the family.
37. Coaxing your wife to tell her secrets.
38. Being divorced from your husband.

FINIS.

Temperance Department.

From the Tunkhannock Republican.

A THANK-OFFERING TO J. T. YARRINGTON.

[NOTE.—These beautiful lines were written by Miss C———, a young lady friend of Mr. J. T. YARRINGTON, of Carbondale, Pa., who is acknowledged and widely known as a zealous and prominent advocate of the Temperance Reform.]

I.

I am not known to thee, nor thou to me,
    Except as those who sing each other know;
Yet thou hast touch'd, unwittingly, the key
    That held my soul's full music; it must flow;
And though its grandeur should fall short of thine,
    It only seeks to thank thee in this strain,
That thou hast shown beneath the purpling wine
    There lies alone the blood-red drops of pain!

II.

That thou hast dar'd to rise above the throng
    Who wreathe the sparkling goblet's edge with flowers;
And who—in empty mirth and ribald song—
    Waste golden moments of their precious hours;
That thou hast dar'd in this most wanton age
    While tempting syrens sing, in thy brave youth,
To turn for glowing eyes that mystic title-page
    Whereon is written TEMPERANCE AND TRUTH!

III.

I well might speak of other brilliant themes
  On which thy pen has dwelt in graceful thought,
Yet 'tis not for thy sweet poetic dreams
  Or eloquence with tender fancies fraught
That I would thank thee most—although they all
  Have held my spirit in a magic spell—
BUT LET ME THANK THEE FOR THE WARNING CALL
  THAT STARTLES HUNDREDS FROM THE VERGE OF HELL!

IV.

Work on: when thy labor of love is done,
  Forgetting the conflict of toil and pain,
Thou shalt receive thanks from many a one
  Whose honor and peace thou hast help'd to gain;
Long may thy voice be lifted 'gainst the wrong,
  The giant wrong that over-rides the earth,
That culls its victims from the sons of song,
  From halls of State, and ranks of noble birth!

V.

Those join'd with thee in the temperance cause,
  May they, too, in well-doing weary not,
Till purg'd our fair escutcheon from such laws—
  Rumselling, its most foul and hateful blot;
. Long may thy hands dash down the chaplet leaves
  That would conceal the poison in the cup,
And while love over fallen manhood grieves,
  O may'st thou hold the sacred banner up!   C.

J. T. YARRINGTON AND THE TEMPERANCE REFORM.

COMMENDATIONS FROM THE PRESS AND PEOPLE.

PERSONAL.

[*From the Scranton Morning Republican.*]

We print elsewhere to-day an able argument advocating independent political action as desirable in the temperance movement. While we do not approve of the project, we are nevertheless willing to give the adherents of the measure a hearing, especially when the plea comes from the pen of one of our own citizens, who is rapidly becoming a prominent and promising leader in the temperance cause.

[*From the New York Daily Times.*]

Mr. J. T. YARRINGTON, of Scranton,* Penn., has published, in the *Republican*, of that city, a paper advocating independent political action to advance the temperance cause.

*Carbondale, Penn.

NEW YORK TRIBUNE, }
NEW YORK, June 28th. }

Mr. J. T. YARRINGTON, Carbondale, Pa.

Dear Sir:—I sympathize very heartily with the efforts you were good enough to bring to my attention, in favor of the temperance cause, and although we may differ as to some details of the movement, we cannot differ at all as to the results aimed at.

With thanks for the courtesy of your letter, I am,
Very respectfully,
(Signed,) WHITELAW REID.

[From the Golden Age, Theodore Tilton, Editor.]

Mr. J. T. YARRINGTON, of Carbondale, Pa., a zealous advocate of the temperance movement, has just received, through the columns of the *Tunkhannock Republican*, a poetical tribute to his useful labors, from the pen of a young Pennsylvania poet of the female sex, whose sign manual is the letter "C."

Mr. YARRINGTON has lately written (not in intoxicating rhymes, but in teetotal prose) an argument in favor of making prohibition the basis of a political party. He approves the views of Hon. Gerrit Smith on this subject. By the way, we shall look to Peterboro for an expression of Mr. Smith's views from his own pen.

HON. GERRIT SMITH TO J. T. YARRINGTON.

The Sentiments of the Pioneer Reformer of America, the Originator of the "Anti-Dramshop Party," on Temperance-Political Suasion.

[Extracts from several Letters.]

Mr. J. T. YARRINGTON, Carbondale, Pa.

Dear Sir:—I have your esteemed letter, and I thank you for the invitation to attend your Grand Temperance Mass Meeting.

I wish I could attend it; but I have not sufficient health to do so.

I trust that you, and my friend, James Black, will go not only for an independent political party, but also for having it confine itself to the one·issue of putting an end to dramselling.

I am an old man (seventy-four,) my health is impaired, and I no longer write much for the press.

And so you are only twenty-three years old ?

God has blessed you with rare wisdom, integrity and firmness—very rare for one so young.

I have just finished reading your "Salutatory." It convinces me that you do not need "a letter of advice" from me. You are quite competent, with the help of your Heavenly Father, to advise yourself.

I have great confidence that God is raising you up to be a rich blessing to your fellow men.

Many thanks for the Scranton *Republican* of June 8th.

· I am glad to see that you are continuing to write so vigorously for our dear cause.

Excuse my brevity. I can give but a few lines to each of my innumerable correspondents.

Heaven bless you !

Very respectfully,

Your friend,

(Signed,) GERRIT SMITH.

Peterboro, N. Y.

LETTER FROM HON. JAMES BLACK, PRESIDENT OF THE PENNSYLVANIA STATE TEMPERANCE UNION.

J. T. YARRINGTON, ESQ., Carbondale, Pa.

Dear Sir and Bro.:—I thank you for your circulars received last week.

The ability and earnestness manifested in these

documents augur great powers of usefulness in the cause of temperance.

How much I admire your heartiness, and the sturdy blows you strike at the monster vice of the age.

I had hoped to meet you and make your acquaintance at the meeting of the State Temperance Union at Harrisburg yesterday, and felt some discontent at having to accept your telegram instead.

I am sorry that I did not become acquainted with you at Gettysburg, and trust that the day is not far distant when we shall strike hands as our hearts are now in fellowship.

* * * * * *

I enclose you a copy of the call to which I referred in my last. If you approve, say how many you can use by forwarding to prominent temperance men who will probably unite in the movement.

Fraternally yours,

(Signed,)   JAMES BLACK.

Lancaster, Pa.

[From the Erie Daily Dispatch.]

Elsewhere are presented some notices of Mr. J. T. YARRINGTON's argument in favor of a special prohibitory party. While we have little sympathy with a project which has a tendency to work disorganization in our own party, we are free to admit that Mr. YARRINGTON has discussed his theme with considerable power and ability.

[From the Record of the Times.]

Our friend, J. T. YARRINGTON, of Carbondale, Pa., is a most industrious man in the temperance cause, and not disposed to hide his light under a bushel.

We have a fresh circular from his pen, with many expressions of opinions from his temperance brethren —not all agreeing with him, by any means,—but commending his zeal and acknowledging his usefulness.

[From the Wyoming Valley Journal.]

We are in receipt of a circular containing an able argument, by J. T. YARRINGTON, of Carbondale, Pa., in favor of forming a National temperance political party.

We are in that boat.

Let the friends of temperance keep the ball rolling.

[From the Carbondale Advance.]

Mr. J. T. YARRINGTON, of this city, is out in another argument in favor of legal suasion over the dram-seller, by prohibition. It is a dispassionate, masterly and energetic article, with no words wasted, and every sentence to the point.

TEMPERANCE AND POLITICS.

Shall we Have a Special Prohibitory Party?

Separate Political Action the Demand of the Hour.

LEGAL SUASION.

An Argument for Practical Prohibition.

BY J. T. YARRINGTON.

REFLECTIONS ON THE COURSE OF ACTION, AS APPLIED TO THE FUTURE OF THE TEMPERANCE CONFLICT, IN RELATION TO MORAL VS. LEGAL SUASION.

OUR NEW CIRCULAR on *"Temperance and Politics"* is now ready for distribution. Let it have a wide circulation. As a temperance campaign document it has been, already, highly endorsed by the press and the people in different parts of the country.

Price, ten cents per copy; six dollars per hundred, by express.

These rates will not much more than pay for printing. Friends of the cause, everywhere, should help to scatter these temperance tracts broadcast, throughout the land.

A FACT.—"Temperance and Politics," by J. T. YARRINGTON, is having a large, extended circulation. Orders are multiplying fast. The demand is from North, South, East and West. "First come, first served!"

Every temperance man and woman in the land should read the article on *Temperance and Politics*, by J. T. YARRINGTON; and those who are *not*, as yet, temperance men and women, should, by all means, read the argument on this important subject, and become at once practical exponents of temperance, total abstinence and legal prohibition. Let us have no more *half-way work* in our temperance ranks !

OUR TRACT on "Temperance and Politics," may be had, in large or small quantities, at the rate of six dollars per hundred;—or, ten cents for a single copy, by mail, postpaid.

Address your orders to J. T. YARRINGTON, Carbondale, Luzerne county, Pennsylvania.

[From the Scranton City Journal.]

*   *   *   *   *   *

Mr. J. T. YARRINGTON is now quite widely known as an apostle of total abstinence, his articles having been published and read in different parts of the country. He has evidently accomplished much good by his writings, as the encomiums he has received from different papers and persons in various localities would seem to indicate.

Many celebrated men have given him words of encouragement and cheer, and his star is in the ascendant. His name is a synonym of temperance and moral reform wherever his writings are known, and we trust he will keep extending his sphere of usefulness until he shall have still more laurels added to his wreath.

Go on, friend YARRINGTON, conquering and to conquer, and may you live to see the dawn of the glorious day of sobriety and peace.

[*From the Worcester Journal.*]

A good cause should be supported by good people. While there are hundreds and thousands of christian men and women in our land who are engaged in, and identified with, the temperance movement, in one way or another; yet there are but few, comparatively, who sacrifice and earnestly labor for the furtherance of this noble reform and the prohibition of the liquor traffic.

We have been led to this reflection since receiving and perusing the article, "Fashionable Intemperance," by our talented and esteemed contributor, J. T. YARRINGTON, which is found in our temperance department to-day.

We are not, as our readers well know, in the habit of "puffing" men and things for selfish or pecuniary motives. Not being acquainted with Mr. YARRINGTON, we know nothing whatever of him as a man or by personal association: but this we do know—that as an able and practical exponent of the righteous cause in which he is so faithfully engaged, J. T. YARRINGTON, of Carbondale, Pa., unquestionably stands among the first leaders in the temperance reformation.

Give us more such defenders of truth and temperance; give us more YARRINGTONS; give us more manly men; give us more daring women; then, and not till then, will we see the triumph of temperance principles.

Long may our temperance workers live to dethrone the power of habit, and may their mantles fall on others to help carry forward the car of progression.

[*From the Tunkhannock Republican.*]

The *Wayne County Herald* editor, under the irritating influence of a whiskey headache, strokes our talented correspondent YARRINGTON's feathers the wrong way.

The *Herald* man is not the only one whom history records as being scared at the writing on the wall. Prohibition means no more "tod" for him. Coming events cast their shadows over him, and he feels all crawly.

YARRINGTON is an able champion of the temperance cause, and we feel proud of him.

_____

[*From the Tuscola American.*]

Among the able defenders of this reform is Mr. J. T. YARRINGTON, of Carbondale, Pennsylvania. His day-star was never brighter; but the glorious future will add to its lustre. He wields the pen of a ready writer, and it is indeed encouraging to find so true a devotee in one so young—for he is scarce more than one-and-twenty.

With a heart in the work, our friend YARRINGTON goes "*right on,*" overcoming the prejudices, obstacles and opposition of all grog-venders, whiskeyites and other enemies.

We predict for this young champion of the temperance cause a great degree of success. Would that we had ten thousand more such, in our ranks, among the young men of our land!

Go on, brother. Let your aspirations be higher! higher! higher! "The pen is mightier than the sword." Continue, then, to use it for God and humanity.

_____

[*From the Temperance Vindicator.*]

It is with pleasure that we publish the following commendatory notice of our friend, Mr. J. T. YARRINGTON, of Carbondale, Pa., from the *Wayne Citizen:*

*   *   *   *   *   *

The fact that this able young champion of the temperance cause has been attacked by the grog-sellers and grog-bruisers in his neighborhood, is an evidence of his efficiency as a temperance advocate.

It is not every one that is willing to incur the enmity of the influential whiskey ring by an open fight with them, for it is known that this hellish power will resort to anything however contemptible and dishonorable, to crush those who dare to do battle for the right and against their infamous business.

Timid, tender-footed policy peddlers, nominal temperance men, do nothings, who blow and bluster when no enemy is in view, but who skulk like guilty things in the presence of liquor-sellers and their thirsty customers, are not subject to the censure of these delectables.

They do not meddle with their neighbors' business!
Of course not.

But it must be conceded that such persons are nobodies—mere cyphers that add not one whit to the great sum of human usefulness.

But when a gentleman of talent has the courage to oppose the traffic in the murder-making fluid, the hyenas who are engaged in the business raise an awful howl, and move the very hills that they may make a grave for his good name, and thus destroy his prestige and weaken his influence in the war against them.

We say to our young co-laborer, go on; strike, right and left, and let the wails of the wounded be music to make you strike more swift and sure.

The right will prevail.

The citizens of Carbondale, and especially those who have fathers and sons likely to be ruined by the curse of intemperance, should be thankful that they have a talented temperance champion among them who has the courage to wage an unrelenting warfare against the enemies of their peace and prosperity.

TOUCH NOT THE SIREN CUP.

A Temperance Dirge.

Touch not the siren cup of death,
  'Tis hell that lurks within;
'Twill give to none good health or breath,
  But trouble, wo and sin!

See the child of sorrow,
  With face so sad and wan,
Comfort seek to borrow
  When hope is almost gone!

Friends strive in vain to cheer
  The soul—for worldly joys
And all the rounds of pleasure here
  Are less than children's toys!

"*List.*"—'Tis the voice of mirth
  Echoing from the bowers
Of the Bacchic sons of earth—
  Oh, what unhallow'd hours!

Such revelry! who can portray?
  Not half the curse is known;—
Who can intemperance subdue, allay,
  And drive the demon from the throne!

Liquor maddens—yes, *worse*, by far:
  It brings the guilty, erring soul
Chargeable at the Judgment Bar,
  God's wrath on it to roll!

Deluded men! oh, hapless slaves!
  How long will you thus tread
Untimely paths to drunkard's graves,
  Your home among the dead!

With Heaven's pure and richest drink
  None shall complain of thirst,
Or fall from lofty station's brink
  To realms of those accurs'd!

Then think, amid your mirth,
  How glory may depart;
The strong are bow'd to earth
  And indurate in heart!

Soon shall the power of fiends and knaves
  Be far remov'd from sight,
And moral, righteous men—not slaves—
  Will battle for the right!

J. T. Yarrington.

THE ABSTAINER'S APPEAL.

BY J. T. YARRINGTON.

He who drinks of the poison'd bowl
  Which FIENDS have drugg'd with hell,
And brings upon his guilty soul
  That horrid, hopeless spell—
Oh, try and reach to him
  A kind, protecting arm :
Repel those shadows dim,
  His careless ways alarm !

The wife a lowly prayer
  May offer by his side,
But a withering sense of shame is there
  Which wounds his manly pride ;
When on such wrecks you gaze
  With pity, tears or sighs,
Then kindly stoop and raise
  The fallen of the skies !

Rains that now are given
  Fall thankless o'er the land,
And another Horeb riven
  Might waste its waves in sand—
For children scorn to bow
  Where parents knelt before,
And cool the weary, burden'd brow
  In rippling springs of yore !

They know not where they stand—
  Strong drink will lead them blind.
Curse their ways, lofty, pure and grand.
  While death at last they find :
We witness here one cause
  Of immorality in man :
God's high and holy laws
  Evade the moral scan !

Total abstainers, one and all,
  Battle on in your might
To rescue souls from such a fall,
  The inebriate's endless night ;
Cause them to dash the siren cup
  Of ruin from their lips,
Lest night should mantle up
  In the spirit's apocalypse !

www.ingramcontent.com/pod-product-compliance
Lightning Source LLC
Chambersburg PA
CBHW030901260626
47169CB00008B/2630